For Patsy, and long overdue — TW-J

Text copyright ©1993 by Tim Wynne-Jones
Illustrations copyright ©1993 by Marie-Louise Gay
First U.S. publication 1994

The publisher gratefully acknowledges the
assistance of the Ontario Arts Council and
Canada Council.

Canadian Cataloguing in Publication Data

Wynne-Jones, Tim.
    The last piece of sky

ISBN 0-88899-181-9

I. Gay, Marie-Louise. II. Title.

PS8595.Y44L38 1993   jC813'.54   C93-093497-0
PZ7.W94La 1993

Library of Congress Cataloguing-in-Publication
Data is available.

A Groundwood Book
Douglas & McIntyre Ltd.
585 Bloor Street West
Toronto, Ontario M6G 1K5

Design by Michael Solomon
Typeset in Stone Informal by Pixel Graphics
Illustrations rendered in pencil, coloured pencil
and dyes on Strathmore watercolour paper
Printed and bound in Hong Kong
by Everbest Printing Co. Ltd.

The Last Piece of Sky

BY Tim Wynne-Jones

PICTURES BY Marie-Louise Gay

A Groundwood Book

Douglas & McIntyre • Toronto Vancouver Buffalo

First Owen walked all over Olivia's
new puzzle.

Olivia hollered. Owen kicked the puzzle
around the room.

Everywhere.

"Help!" said Olivia.

"Why should I?" said Owen.

"I'll never find it all!" said Olivia.

"I'm going out to my tree," said Owen.

Owen's tree stood on the bank of Heartbeat Pond. He stood under its weeping branches. He hurled a rock at the pond. Splash! A duck quacked noisily at him.

"What you want," said the duck, "is a talk with the snake."

"I don't want anything," said Owen.

"Quack," said the duck. "Follow me."
"Why should I?" said Owen. But he
followed all the same.

The duck circled a lone bulrush in the very centre of Heartbeat Pond.

"Quack," said the duck. "Pull it."

"Why should I?" said Owen. But he pulled all the same.

Hard.

Harder. And harder still. Until…

Schlop! It came out.

What was going on? His boat was sinking!
The whole pond was sinking!

Soon Owen sat in his boat, in the mud, on the floor of Heartbeat Pond. There was a house there — its walls wet with weeds, its roof greasy with slime, its windows slick with swampgrass stain.

"Quack," said the duck. "Knock on the door."
"Why should I?" said Owen.
But he knocked.

The door oozed open. Owen stepped inside. In the gloom sat a stone table. And at the stone table stood a single stone chair. And sitting in the chair was a green snake sipping pond scum from a heavy stone goblet.

"I suppose you're looking for a little piece of sky," said the snake.

"I'm not looking for anything," said Owen.

"Very well," said the snake. "Then you won't be much interested in finding a place that is high and wide."

"Why would I want to talk to a snake?" said Owen.

"Why should I care about a little piece of sky?" said Owen.

"Why would I want to find a place that is high and wide?" said Owen. "Wherever that is."

"It's closer than you think," said the snake. "But first you need to get to the bottom of this. Follow me."

And before Owen could say "Why should I?" the snake dipped its green head right into the goblet of pond scum and then followed — its whole, long, green, slippery body slithering, slithering, slithering…

And disappearing with a flick of its green tail.

Owen was utterly alone.

He gazed into the goblet. It didn't look very appetizing.

"I'm not a snake!" said Owen. His reflection in the pond scum stared back at him. "Hey, come back here," he yelled.

But the snake did not come back.

Owen thought very hard. "There must be some other way to get to the bottom of this."

He thought again — harder this time and deeper, too. It was some kind of riddle. "How could there be a place high and wide at the bottom of a goblet of pond scum?"

"Hmmm," he thought again, a third time, so that his thinking voice filled the little house on the floor of Heartbeat Pond. And he got a bright idea.

"Maybe if I spill it all out," he thought.

Slowly, because it was very full, Owen lifted the stone goblet. It took all his might. How would he ever carry such a heavy thing outdoors, because he knew he couldn't spill it inside. Up it came. Up, up…

Then something caught his eye. Something at the very bottom of the goblet — under it, in fact. And it *was* something high and wide — a little piece of sky.

Owen put down the goblet.

He could hardly believe his eyes.

"A little piece of sky," he cried.

Back in his boat, the sky safe in his pocket,
Owen put the plug back in. Heartbeat Pond
filled up again.

And when he got home — sure enough —
it was the only piece of the puzzle missing.
Olivia even let him put it in.